10 CATS

Emily Gravett

TWO HOOTS

10
cats

1
white cat

2
black cats

3
cats with stripes

4
cats with patches

5
cats with
red spots

6
cats with
yellow dots

7
cats with
blue blotches

8
cats with
orange splotches

9
cats with
green splats

10
multicoloured
cats